goose

MOLLY BANG

THE BLUE SKY PRESS

An Imprint of Scholastic Inc. · New York

THE BLUE SKY PRESS

Library of Congress Cataloging-in-Publication Data

Bang, Molly.

Goose/written and illustrated by Molly Bang.

p.   cm.

Summary: Adopted by woodchucks at birth, a baby goose never

feels she truly belongs—until the day she discovers she can fly.

ISBN 0-590-89005-0

(1. Geese — Fiction.   2. Woodchuck — Fiction.

3. Identity — Fiction.)   I. Title.

PZ7.B2217Go 1996 (E) — dc20   95-47616   CIP   AC

12 11 10 9 8 7 6 5 4 3   7 8 9/9 0 1/0

Printed in the United States of America   37

First printing, September 1996

Production supervision by Angela Biola

Designed by Molly Bang and Kathleen Westray

TO MY GOOSE

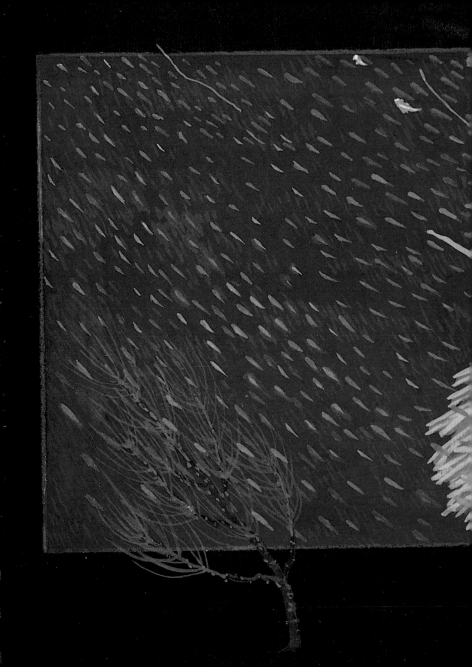

On a dreadfully dark and stormy night,

an egg was blown right out of its nest.

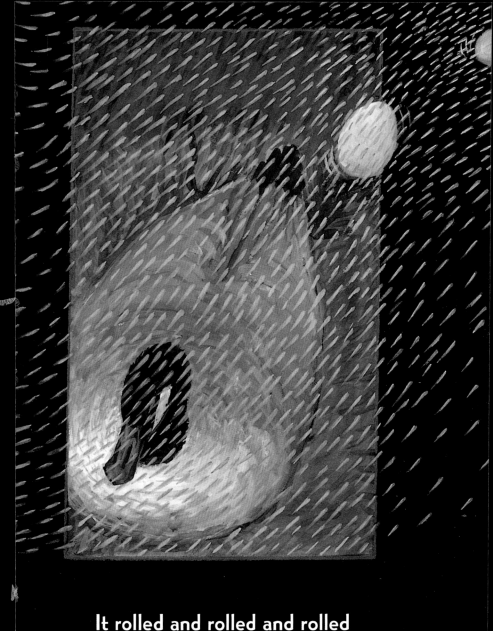

It rolled and rolled and rolled

down a deep, deep hole,

until it landed in a den of woodchucks

where a baby goose hatched out!

That baby goose was adored
by her new brothers and sisters and
by her new momma and poppa,

who taught her everything they thought
a youngster should know.

And that little goose

learned very, very well.

But the goose was often sad.

She felt different from everyone else,
and nothing could make her feel better.

Her family tried to make her happy,

but they couldn't.

Her friends tried to make her happy,

but **THEY** couldn't.

So the goose set off into the world

to see what she could figure out by herself.

Things only got worse—and worse.

All alone, the goose felt sadder and sadder.

She was so lonely,

she didn't notice where she was going.
She lost her footing—

and fell!

Down, down, down she dropped.

falling toward the ocean below.

Fighting to stay aloft,

she flailed

and flapped her wings,

and found out—

she could FLY!

So she flew and flew and flew,

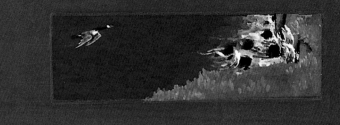

all the way home.

You know, that goose
surprised everyone,
especially herself.